To
Jordan

Feb. 14, 2015

Dear Jordan,
      Happy Valentine's Day, Jordan.
We love you soooo much. Have
a great day.
      I met the author of this
book, and he signed it for you. Have
fun reading it with Isak.
                    Love,
            ♡  Mormor
                  + Papa
                  XOXO
                  2016

# The Mouse

## and the

# Cuckoo

Written by Keith Lawrence Roman

Illustrated by Barbara Litwiniec

The Mouse and the Cuckoo
Morningside Books Hardcover Edition
Copyright © 2016 Keith Lawrence Roman
All rights reserved.
Published in the United States of America by
Morningside Books, Orlando, Florida

This edition is cataloged as:
ISBN 978-1-945044-02-1
MorningsideBooks.net

Printed in China

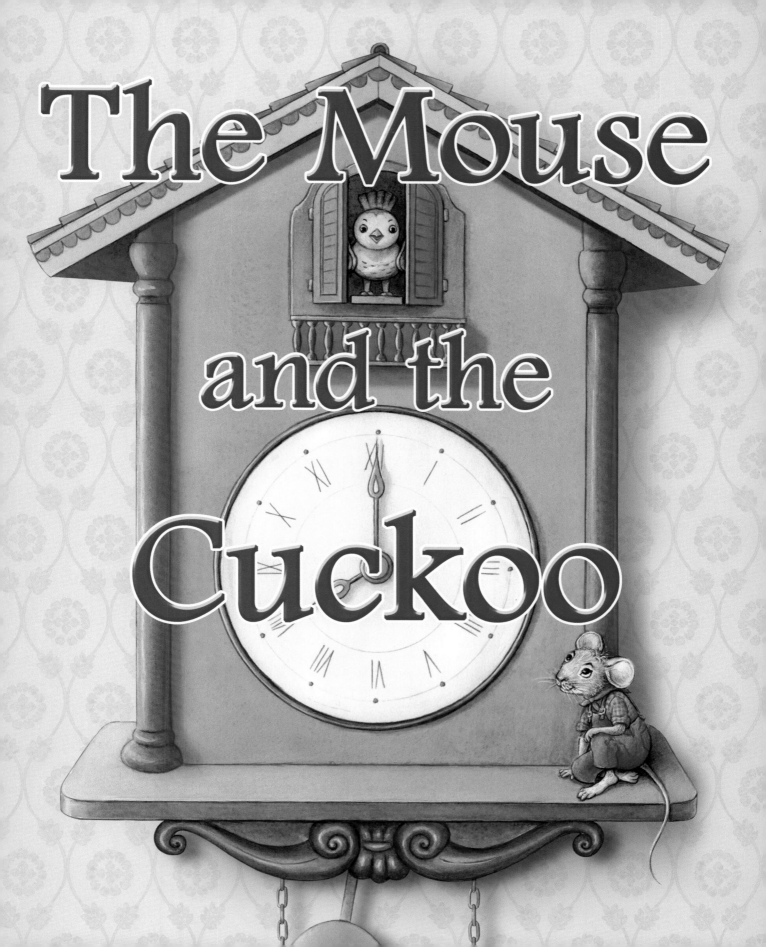

# The Mouse and the Cuckoo

Once upon a moment past
there lived a little mouse,
Who everyday climbed up a chain
to reach a little house.

For in that house
there lived a friend,
a tiny little bird,
Who never had too much to say,
but wanted to be heard.

The bird would pop right into view,
     from two small wooden doors.
And speak out loud "Coo koo, Coo koo,"
     then leave and say no more.

As quickly as she sang her chime,
she soon was in her house.
And waiting for another time
alone there sat the mouse.

Every hour, on the hour, the little bird appeared.
And every hour her friend the mouse
would climb up to be near.

The mouse would greet her
with a smile,
as nicely as can be.

"Might you stop and talk awhile,
        would you,
            could you, please?"

But the Cuckoo never stopped,
just came and left its cheer.
The mouse then thought the bird was deaf,
the Cuckoo could not hear.

The mouse began to scream at her,
and wave his arms about.
"Can't you understand me?"
His voice became a shout!

Never did the Cuckoo once
offer a reply.
She said her quick
"Coo koo Coo koo,"
and left without goodbye.

Next the mouse decided that the Cuckoo must not care.
"Why else would she ignore me, as if I wasn't there?"

Inside the Cuckoo's heart there lived
a singing little bird,
but she could only speak each day
the same two little words.

How could she ever find a way
to let her dear mouse know,
With all her heart
she longed to say,
how much she
loved him so.

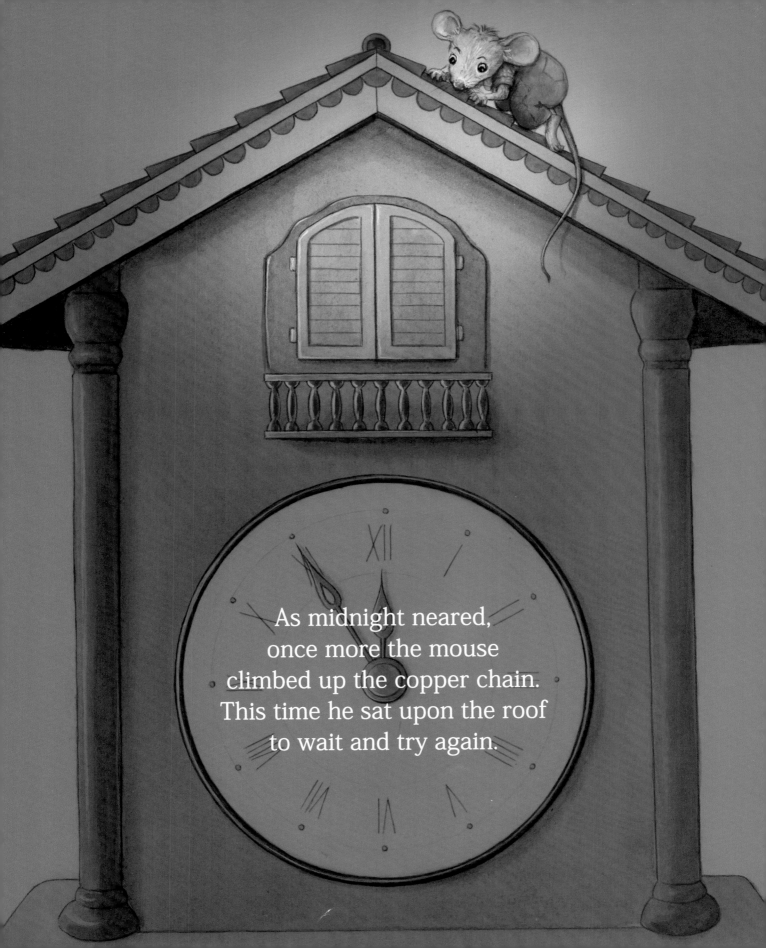

As midnight neared,
once more the mouse
climbed up the copper chain.
This time he sat upon the roof
to wait and try again.

The midnight chime
was longer and the
Cuckoo stayed outside.

The mouse jumped
down into the house,
in darkness there to hide.

Coo    koo  Coo  koo

After twelve Coo koo Coo koos,
The doors slammed closed and locked.
The mouse and little bird were left
alone inside the clock.

Finally a chance, he thought, to tell her how I feel.
Here in the dark, alone at last, her heart she will reveal.

The little mouse then chirped and squeaked,
"I love you dear Cuckoo."
And in the dark was sure he heard,
    "Dear Mouse, I love you too."

Coo koo Coo koo her only words,
then and again she said.
The little mouse took this to mean,
"It's late and time for bed."

So for that hour from twelve to one
the mouse and bird took rest.
But all too soon the time had come
for one to leave their nest.

Coo koo! Coo koo! the Cuckoo said,
"The time is one o'clock."
Stand back, my dearest little mouse.
The doors will now unlock."

The doors were sprung, the Cuckoo flew
by force into the light,
But fastened to the little stage
was drawn back to the night.

Once again inside the clock,
          the Cuckoo's words were clear.
If only for an hour more,
          her voice the mouse could hear.

"Coo koo Coo koo," The Cuckoo said, "I want so to be free.
But I am fastened to the clock. Won't you please help me?"

At her feet the Cuckoo bird
was shackled with a lock.
Forever she would have to live
inside the wooden clock.

The mouse began to chew and gnaw
the chain around her feet.
But brass and steel will never yield
to mice with just their teeth.

Through the night and through the dawn,
the two of them were spoons.
They talked and dreamed the hours away,
until the clock struck noon.

Then the Cuckoo did her dance
and sang twelve Coo koos more.

The little mouse then took his chance
and scampered through the doors.

"Coo koo Coo koo," the Cuckoo said,
"Goodbye my friend, Goodbye."
And as a single teardrop shed,
her song became a sigh.

Climbing down the chain
the mouse looked back
to see his friend,
Sadly singing out Coo koo
for years without an end.

He called to her,
his truest love,
and though she
could not hear,

He promised to
himself and her
and all that he
held dear!

"Dear Cuckoo, hold still your heart, for I will set you free.
One day soon I will return, and bring with me a key."

The Cuckoo sang
a thousand chimes,
a year had slowly passed.

And after all
the Cuckoo's rhymes,
the mouse returned at last.

His promise kept,
the mouse returned
to free her from her jail.

He climbed the chain
a final time, the key
held by his tail.

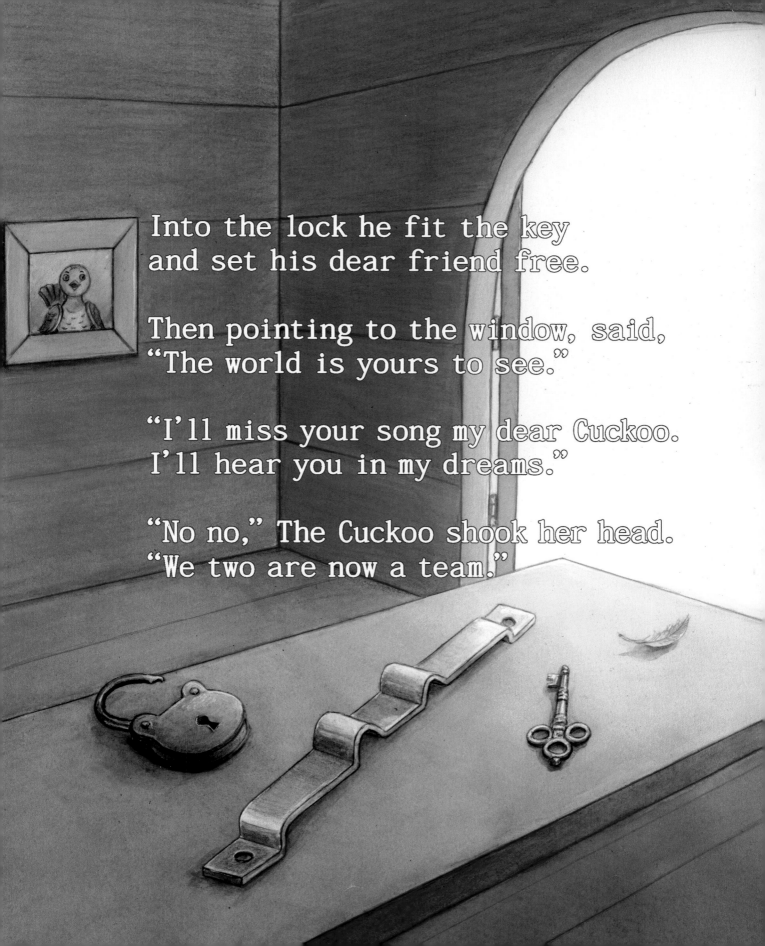

Into the lock he fit the key
and set his dear friend free.

Then pointing to the window, said,
"The world is yours to see."

"I'll miss your song my dear Cuckoo.
I'll hear you in my dreams."

"No no," The Cuckoo shook her head.
"We two are now a team."

"Coo koo Coo koo," the Cuckoo said.

"Together we will be.

"Climb upon my back, dear mouse.

and fly away with me."